COLD WAR
A Sgt Major Crane Cold Case
Book 3

By

Wendy Cartmell

Table of Contents

By Wendy Cartmell

Wendy Cartmell is a bestselling Amazon author, well known for her chilling crime thrillers. These include the Sgt Major Crane mysteries, Crane and Anderson police procedurals, the Emma Harrison mysteries and a cozy mystery series, set in Muddlebay. Further, a psychic detective series has been written, the first of which, Touching the Dead has been followed by six further books in the series. Finally, the haunted series is a collection of ghostly happenings in buildings or objects. Just click the covers to go to the book pages on Amazon.

Sgt Major Crane crime thrillers:

Crane and Anderson crime thrillers:

Emma Harrison mysteries

Supernatural suspense

Cozy mystery

Cold Cases

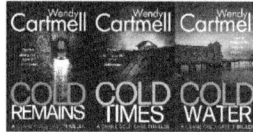

All my books are available to purchase or borrow from Amazon by clicking the covers or entering Amazon HERE.

Cold Water

When a skeleton is found in the Basingstoke Canal, death appears to be a single gunshot wound to the head, that was found lying nearby.

Dog tags and DNA tests confirm the body is Sgt Green, a soldier from Aldershot Garrison. A soldier whose child, Max, has also disappeared. He has never been found. It was generally thought at the time, that Green had absconded with the child.

So why was Sgt Green killed?

And as there were no other remains found in the canal, where is Max?

Prologue

Mavis looked out of the window of their cottage and waived gaily as her husband and son drove off. They were going to the cinema in Douglas to see Wonka, the remake of Charlie and the Chocolate Factory movie. But as soon as her family were out of the way, her face fell and she poured herself a cup of black coffee from the machine in the kitchen. She wandered outside and sat on a bench in the sunshine. She should be happy. She lived in a lovely house, which was truly a family home. Her husband had a good job, and her son was doing well in school. But there was something wrong with her boy and she was having difficulty putting her finger on the reason.

It had begun a couple of months ago. He started having night terrors and she would find him staring out of his bedroom window and screaming. He frequently shouted, 'No, no, don't, I won't,' but she has no idea why or what it could mean. Last night he was thrashing about in bed, and it was very difficult to control him. It was like he was having some sort of seizure, lashing out at her when she tried to put her arms around him. She was bruised black and blue by him hitting her this week.

But what really worried her was what he'd said over breakfast the next day.

'Are the tanks coming back today, Mummy?'

'Daddy needs to be careful with that rifle, doesn't he?'

'When will Daddy be back from exercise? I really miss him,' and his eyes had filled with tears.

She thought her heart was going to burst at that one. She had no idea what he was talking about, as her husband had just left for work. It really was very confusing and upsetting, for all of them, not just her. Her boy was becoming more and more emotionally unstable, and she truly didn't know what to do about it.

Unbidden, the tears began trickling down her face. She'd had to be so strong and not show any emotion in front of either her son or her husband. But once on her own there was no reason for restraint, and she could let go of the stranglehold on her emotions. Pulling her laptop towards her, she entered the website of her doctor's surgery and asked for an appointment, despite her misgivings. In the meantime, she'd try the suggestions on the NHS website.

During a night terror, you should stay calm and wait for the person to calm down.

Do not talk to them or try to stop them moving about, unless there's a risk they could hurt themselves or someone else.

Do not try to wake them – they may not recognise you and may get more upset if you try to comfort them.

And the final one was if they're having a night terror at the same time every night, try waking them up 15 minutes before the night terror every night for a week. This can sometimes stop the night terrors happening.

Well, she'd already tried all of those and nothing had changed. He was still having terrors. And, of course, her husband wasn't any help at all. He didn't even wake up! Worse than useless, she grumbled to herself.

Anyway, all the introspection wouldn't get the washing done or the bathroom cleaned and reluctantly she pulled herself out of the chair and went to the bathroom to get the washing basket. She could only hope her GP could help. If he couldn't, and the cause was that unspeakable thing they never talked about, then she'd go mad with worry.

For constantly looking over their shoulders was no way to live a life.

Chapter 1

The weather had turned. Gone was the rain and mild weather and Aldershot was now in the grip of a fierce cold spell. But the change was welcome to Anne Smith as she walked alongside the Basingstoke Canal. The earth beneath her feet was firm, covered by a layer of crisp frost. Her breath floated around her like gossamer. At her feet walked her best friend. Paddy was an aging golden labrador and Anne couldn't bear to think that one day he would be gone and leave her all alone.

Her musings were interrupted by a flurry of furious barking from Paddy. He had stopped at the edge of the canal, barking at something that appeared to be in the water. It was unusual for the dog to bark at all, so Anne stooped to investigate. Holding Paddy's lead tightly in her hand, she knelt next to her dog and scanned the water trying to see what had upset him. It was probably some creature. As she calmed the dog by stroking him and whispering sweet nothings, he suddenly began barking again. Something was definitely upsetting him in the water.

As Anne leaned over to see what it was, a dull grey something bobbed in the water. As it twisted and turned it became obvious what it was. Stifling a scream, she stood and backed away from the canal, dragging Paddy with her.

Scrabbling for her phone she rang 999.

'Police please,' she managed to say. 'I've just seen a human skull in the Basingstoke Canal at Ash Lock. There's a hole in the forehead, as though whoever it was, was shot.'

Chapter 2

Out with Daniel, Crane was still thinking about the conviction of John Berry, his last case, and he grinned.

'What are you grinning about, Dad?'

'It's nice to have your mates around you, isn't it?'

Daniel nodded.

'Well, it's nice for me to have mine as well.'

'Who are your mates, then Dad? I've got Jimmy from my class. David from football. Evan from swimming. And Clarisa from next door.'

Crane nodded. 'That's a good bunch of people you have there.'

'So, who are yours, Dad?'

'Billy, Dudley-Jones, Padre Symmonds and Kim, oh and Derek Anderson.'

'So, nothing's changed then?' said Daniel.

Out of the mouth of babes and children thought Crane. 'No, Daniel, you're right, nothing's changed.'

As they climbed out of the car Crane's mobile rang.

'Ah, good afternoon, Sgt Major. Bevins from Aldershot police here, Sir.'

'Hi, Bevins. What can I do for you? We won, remember, so surely there's nothing wrong.'

'Ah, well, it's just that a body has been found.'

Crane's stomach sank. 'And?'

'Well, more of a skeleton, really. It was found in the canal.'

'What has it to do with me?'

'It looks like he's been shot in the head.'

'Again, what has that to do with me?'

'We also found a set of dog tags lodged in the mud underneath him. Looks like he was a soldier. So, we might just have found another one of your cold cases.'

Chapter 3

Sgt Bevins shivered. The day hadn't seemed to warm up at all and he looked as if he was suffering badly, despite his overcoat covering his police uniform. Stamping his feet and blowing into his hands, Crane saw him begin walking up and down the tow path. Turning, he saw Crane walking towards him and raised an arm in greeting.

'What on earth?' Crane said. 'A skeleton?'

'Yes,' agreed Bevins. 'Wearing these,' and he held out a plastic bag, which contained dog tags.

There were two round stainless steel discs. Engraved on each of them were:

O POS

24355246

GREEN

M A

C E

Translated to his blood group; O Positive. His army number, surname, initials and religion, in this case Church of England.

Crane had to agree with Bevins. The skeleton was potentially a soldier called M.A. Green. Shit. 'Where were they found?'

'Tangled on one of the bones on the bottom of the canal. We've got divers down there. We're hoping not to have to drain the canal. All sorts of toxic gases could be released from the silt at the bottom, apparently. The waterways people are apoplectic. They want us out of here as soon as possible, but we won't be going anywhere until we recover as many bones as we can.'

'OK, let me take a photo of the tags and then I can pull his records. Let's see if his file marries this. I'll just see Major Martin and then be on my way.'

Crane walked over to the canal bank where the Home Office Pathologist Major Martin (retired) was laying out the bones as they were recovered by the divers.

'Morning, Major,' Crane said. 'How are you?'

'Cold but glad it's not raining, I suppose. Come to see my bones, have you?' and the Major clambered to his feet, his suit crackling alarmingly. 'We've found quite a bit of him. What do you think?'

Crane looked at the bones. 'To be honest, I don't think anything. To me it's a load of bones, but to you? Well, that's a different matter. What are they telling you?'

Major Martin grinned. 'Potentially I have the skeleton of a tall male, I'll know if he's had old injuries and stuff once I get them back to base.'

'Any idea how long he's been in there?'

'Say four to five years at a guess for now.'

'Will you be able to get DNA?'

'Oh, I'll certainly try. It's not impossible.'

'That will help with a positive ID,' said Crane.

'Of course. I'll keep you posted.'

'Thanks, Major,' said Crane wandering back to Bevins.

'Right, I'm off,' he said. 'I've left Daniel with the au pair, so I'll go back to barracks and check up on Green. I'll let you know what I find.'

Chapter 4

Back at Provost Barracks, Crane grabbed a coffee, then fired up his computer. He inputted Green's details into the search function. It didn't take long for the machine to do its stuff and the results were startling. Green wasn't just any old cold case. It had been a red-hot case in its time. A lost soldier and a lost four year old boy. The case dragged on for over a year, before being scaled back and neither Green, nor his son, had ever been found. Until now, it seemed.

Crane pushed away from his desk. His eyes were hurting from reading the screen, so he set the printer going, so he would have a paper copy of all the documents. While it was printing, he started his whiteboard. What he wanted to do first of all was to establish a timeline.

The board was still in the unoccupied room where he'd laid out the files in the John Berry case. As no one had commented on his use of the room, Crane was inclined to use it again for the Green investigation. He went past Dudley-Jones' desk to the half-hidden door and the room which ran the length of the barracks. He set up three tables and cleaned the whiteboard. He started this in between trips to the printer to bring in the pages of the file.

The salient points were that Sgt Sam Green left home with Max about 8.30 am on the 1st September, which was to be Max's first day at school in the Reception class. Only he never arrived. Green and Max had left in Green's car, as he was supposed to be going to work once Max was safely ensconced in school. He also never arrived.

The last sighting of Green had been at 8.45am when his car was caught on a CCTV camera leaving the garrison via Allison Road. Thornhill Road would have led him to Government Road and onwards to Ash Lock. A journey of just over a mile.

As his remains had been found there, it was natural to surmise that was the end of Green's journey. But possibly just the beginning of Max's, as he had never been found. It was generally thought at the time that Green had absconded with the child. But that looked unlikely now as there were no other remains found in the canal.

Crane took photographs printed from the file and pinned them to his board. Sgt Green was a weatherbeaten, dour Yorkshire man aged 38, attached to an Infantry Regiment. He had been a Training Sergeant, bringing the raw recruits up to a predetermined level of competence, so they could pass out and become fully fledged members of the British Army. He was married to Johanne and they had lived on the Garrison in an army quarter.

Max had been a happy child by all accounts and had joined in playgroups and the occasional creche on the Garrison. He played with the children near his house and was an enthusiastic regular at the local playground. He had a cheeky grin and long blond hair that framed his face with ringlets. He was a beautiful child and Crane could see that he might well be the envy of a childless couple, or even traffickers, or God forbid paedophiles. But if that were the case, how did such people firstly find Max and secondly, how had they duped Sgt Green into giving him up?

Crane also printed out a map taken from the internet, showing the route from the Garrison to Ash Lock where Sam Green's remains were found. It was a straightforward drive of literally a few minutes. Once at the lock, the land was flat with uninterrupted views along the canal. Green could have feasibly pulled off the road and taken the short path to the lock. It was an unmanned lock and if there were no boats on the canal in that area, then he and Max wouldn't have been seen. And if they had, what was wrong with a father and his boy out near the water?

He would have been in full sight of the road, but of course they had no idea what cars or lorries would have been in the vicinity four or five years ago. Nevertheless, Crane would ask Diane Chambers to put out a call for witnesses in her article covering the find.

She wouldn't be able to resist the story. He could see it now. In the no doubt lurid article, she would scream, *Why was Sgt Green killed? And where is Max?*

She may get wind of a few explanations that could work and might help Crane. But he was in no doubt that mostly the responses would be dross and do nothing but delay his investigation. But still, he had to try.

The phone interrupted Crane's musings. It was Bevins. 'We've traced the widow, Mrs Johanne Green. Do you want to come with me to tell her about her husband?'

Stupid question. Of course he would.

Chapter 5

From the file, Crane saw the mother, Johanne Green, had been forced out of her army quarter and now rented a small two bedroomed apartment over a shop on the ignominiously named High Street. It was more of an abandoned street in the town, full of take-aways and closed shops. The flats over them seemed to be in as bad order as the boarded-up establishments and it was to one of these that Crane was led, with his new-found partner, Sgt Bevins.

Crane spied a bell next to a very small front door, wedged in-between two empty shops. He shuddered at the thought of cockroaches or rats. Still, needs must, and he pushed the bell. A few beats later it was opened on the chain by what at first glance appeared to be an elderly woman.

'Yes?'

'Mrs Green? Mrs Johanne Green?'

'Who wants to know?'

Crane felt as though he were in a bad crime movie. 'Sgt Major Crane, Provost Barracks. Could I talk to you for a moment please?'

Before she could say no, Bevins moved to within her eyesight, his uniform on full display, complete with crackling radio. 'Please, Mrs Green, you don't want to do this on the street.'

Without further ado, Mrs Green pushed the door to, unhooked the chain and walked up the stairs. Following her, Crane saw musty old carpet, fraying at the edges with the distinct smell of cat pee.

As they walked into her flat, she entered what was probably the living room. She sat in a large armchair, which was obviously her normal seat, surrounded as it was by a full ashtray, a wine glass full of red liquid and a half empty wine bottle.

Johanne Green herself was a woman weighed down with grief if ever there was one. Although in her 40's she looked much older, lank grey hair framing a face devoid of make-up and a shaking hand as she lifted her glass. Although it was after 6 pm on a Saturday night, Crane got the feeling this was how she spent all her nights. Or maybe she was just having a bad day. Who knew? But if she wasn't having a bad day, she was about to.

'Mrs Green,' Bevins said gently, 'We've found remains in the Basingstoke Canal at Ash Lock.'

Crane watched her skin go greyer.

'We believe they are the remains of your husband, Sam Green.'

'And Max?' she asked, leaning forward and grabbing the arms of her chair.

'We've found nothing else.'

Crane opened his mouth then shut it. He was going to say he was sorry. But for what? He wondered if they should be sorry they didn't find any more remains. No one wanted the child to be dead. But if his remains weren't there, then where was he? Wasn't that a reason for hope?

'But I thought that bastard had taken Max and left me. Abducted him. If he's dead, well where the hell is Max then?'

'Exactly. That's what Bevins and I are going to try and establish.'

'Who the fuck are you anyway?'

Crane recoiled from her anger. 'Military Police.'

'Thought so. You've the look. Your lot never found him first time round. Why should now be any different?'

'I work the military cold cases. It's what I do. I'm going to have a shot at finding out what happened. Will you help me? Answer my questions?'

'Oh very well. I've no choice. I want my boy back.' Tears tracked down her cheeks unchecked.

'What do you still have of your husband's possessions? Phone or laptop? Notebooks? Papers?'

'All of it is still here. No one was interested. They just thought that he was gone and that was the end of it. Everyone assumed he'd just left me and taken Max. I hated Sam for it. Still do. And now I find the stupid bastard got himself killed.'

Crane listened to her growing anger without comment.

'I had a home once, you know. Then that got taken away from

me too. No one has cared for over four years, so excuse me if I don't fall at your feet in adoration. Sam's stuff is upstairs in the wardrobe in a cardboard box in the spare room. Help yourself.'

She knocked back her drink and went to light a cigarette. Bevins went upstairs and Crane waited in the hall. When Bevins returned, Crane moved back into the room and thanked Mrs Green.

'Oh, by the way, do you remember any passwords Sam used for his phone or laptop?'

The look she threw him said it all. It was a fuck off look if ever there was one. But then her face crumbled in on itself and she began to sob. 'Find Max,' she said. 'Please, please find him and bring him home.'

Crane had no words, so as she looked at him imploringly, he gave a stiff nod, then turned away and left the flat behind Bevins. He could only hope that Dudley-Jones could work his magic on the laptop and phone.

Outside, Bevans handed the box to Crane. 'Will your lot deal with this?'

'Of course, glad to,' said Crane, hoping to God Billy agreed. 'I'll take it back to the Barracks, then jump on it Monday morning when everyone is in, and I can enlist the help of Dudley-Jones.'

'I'll bid you goodnight, then,' said Bevans before striding back up the street in the direction of Aldershot Police Station.

Chapter 6

On Monday morning, Crane stopped at Billy's office when he arrived at work.

'Morning, Boss,' he said, after tapping on the open door. 'Got a new case. Well, a new cold case.'

'Oh yes?' Billy looked up from the papers he was reading.

Crane quickly explained about finding the remains of Sgt Sam Green.

'I remember that one,' said Billy. 'What about the kid? What was his name?'

'Max,' said Crane.

'Of course, anything on him?'

Crane shook his head. 'I'm afraid not. The only remains were adult ones. Major Martin is checking them out and should be able to get DNA from the bones. But it's reasonably safe to assume it's Sgt Green. The police retrieved his dog tags.'

Billy nodded, clearly thinking. 'Very well,' he said eventually. 'Run with it and see what happens. Who's your police liaison on this?'

'Sgt Bevins. DI Wood seems to have pulled strings and is happy for Bevins to work with me when I need police back-up or information that only they can get.'

'What's your next move?'

'We've got personal effects from the widow, Johanne Green, including a mobile and a laptop. Can I use Dudley-Jones?'

'Sure. Let's hope he gets something worthwhile.'

'Thanks, Boss,' said Crane and melted away. Although Billy was to all intents and purposes his boss, Crane pretty much acted with autonomy. Which suited Crane just fine. One thing he couldn't abide was someone looking over his shoulder and commenting on his handling of a case. He didn't want Billy looking too closely, as sometimes Crane ignored both procedure and orders. He would rather Billy be able to truthfully say he had no idea that Crane would do such a thing. Crane grinned, heading over to Dudley-Jones.

'Morning DJ,' Crane said cheerfully. 'Got a present for you.'

'Ah, Crane,' Dudley-Jones said. 'You're in a good mood, which means a new case for you and a shed load of work for me.'

Crane's grin widened. 'You know you love it, DJ. I've got presents for you,' and he handed over the laptop and mobile phone.

Dudley-Jones looked at them disdainfully. 'Where the hell did you get these from?' he said. 'They look like they've come out of the ark.'

'Not quite, but they are at least four years old.'

'And the rest,' Dudley-Jones grumbled.

'Never mind, it's just the sort of project that you love,' and Crane went onto tell him about Sgt Sam Green and Max Green.

'Very well. Does…?'

'Yes, Dudley-Jones, Billy knows and said you could help me.'

'Bugger, I was hoping to get out of it,' he mumbled under his breath as Crane walked away.

But Crane heard him all the same and grinned.

The following morning, Dudley-Jones wandered into the Cold Case Office, as Crane had taken to calling it.

'Right, Crane, got a minute?'

'For you, always,' Crane said and gestured to an empty chair. 'So, what have you got for me?'

'Not much, I'm afraid. I've done a dump of calls and texts but only one thing stands out. A call from a private number from the phone records.'

'A cold call?' said Crane.

'Yes and no. Not necessarily, as he spoke to someone there at length I reckon. Over 10 minutes anyway. That's a long time for a cold call.'

'It was someone he knew.'

'I think so as well,' said Dudley-Jones.

'But you can't trace the call?'

'No, sorry. But then there's his laptop.'

'Yes?' said Crane with hope in his voice.

'Well, it looks like he was looking at a website about a school.'

'A school? What? For Max?'

'I guess,' said Dudley-Jones.

'That sounds very non-committal. OK which one is it? Do you have it loaded?'

'Not exactly. It seems it's no longer there. I've managed to pull up some ghost screenshots. But the website isn't up any longer.'

'Are you telling me the school wasn't real?'

'Who knows, Crane? That's your area of expertise. I can only tell you what I found, it's up to you to deduce anything from it. Here,' he said handing a small metallic object to Crane. 'This is everything I could find on Green's computer.'

Chapter 7

Before he did that, Crane rang Johanne Green and asked her if she remembered any talk about a school.

'Well, we'd been talking about it. We could have had help with school fees, if we wanted Max to go to boarding school in England, as we were having to move to Germany. But I thought Max was too young and I didn't want anything to do with the stupid idea.'

Crane could hear the disdain in her voice. For the idea? Or just for her husband? He wasn't sure as yet. Maybe both.

'Do you think he might have gone ahead with the plan on his own?'

'No idea.'

Then silence. A silence that worried Crane.

'Mrs Green, I'm sorry to ask but were you two getting on?'

There was a heartfelt sigh. 'Not really. It was hard being an army wife. Maybe if I was the type to say yes Sir no Sir three bags full Sir. But I wasn't. So, we fought each other at every turn. Max. Moving. Him going away. When I was alone, I did as I pleased. When he came home, we had to do it his way, which caused a lot of friction.'

Crane nodded to himself. It was a recurring theme. How hard it was being an army wife with a husband that bounced in and out of their lives. And how undervalued they always were by the army. And if their partner was killed? Then they not only lost a husband and father, but also their home as well if they lived in an army quarter.

Crane was beginning to wonder if they should be looking at Johanne Green for having something to do with her husband's death. But she had been prodded and poked, their home turned upside down, and no evidence had been found that she might have been involved in a plot to kill her husband.

'What? What have you found out?' snapped Johanne Green.

'Nothing as yet, Mrs Green. I'm just bouncing around a few

ideas. Obviously, I'll let you know if I find any evidence as to where Max has gone.'

As Crane replaced the receiver, he inserted the small memory stick into his computer. He had to really stare into the screen to see anything. It was like looking at a photograph bathed in fog with only the vaguest suggestion of a building in it. As he flicked through the six images, different parts of the building swam into view, but it was hard to get an overall impression of the school, if that's what it was, from them. There was a headline, 'Welcome to...' but the remainder of the text had disappeared. The building looked like a stately home, but then a lot of the private schools looked like one. Or indeed once were. Dudley-Jones had done a reverse image search but that hadn't helped any either.

Just then Dudley-Jones crashed through the door. 'Crane, I've got it. There was a screenshot on Green's computer, come and see.'

Crane hurried out of the office, to peer over the shoulder of Dudley-Jones. And there it was. A shot of the front of a stately home and the words, 'Welcome to Pierpoint School.'

'Does it exist?'

'Not that I can find out. But then again Green wouldn't have questioned it. There was a large website, remember.'

Crane nodded. 'Where is this fictional school, does it say?'

'The Isle of Man.'

'So,' said Crane, thinking out loud. 'What if someone lured Green in. Talked about an amazing boarding school on the Isle of Man he could send his son to, that the army would pay for, as Green was due to move to Germany? Let me see what his oppos say.'

Chapter 8

From the details of the original investigation, Crane found the names of three close friends. After searching the military records, he found that one, Sgt Reg Brown was back on Aldershot Garrison and so Crane set out to find him.

Reg Brown was still training young recruits and at that particular moment was teaching them how to march. Without much success. Crane wasn't sure he'd seen such a bloody mess in all his army career. Floppy arms were swinging wildly, and torsos stooped without any backbone to them. Feet were tripping over each other and over the boots in front. It looked like every set of legs were out of time and out of step with their neighbour's. All in all, a bloody mess, which no doubt contributed to the sour look on Sgt Brown's face.

Taking the safest route along the outside of the parade ground, Crane approached Brown, who looked glad of the interruption. Leaving the men in the safe hands of a colleague, Crane drew him away and introduced himself, commenting that he was investigating the death of Sgt Sam Green.

'Death? Sam?'

'Yes, I'm afraid so. His remains were found in the Basingstoke Canal.'

'The canal? He didn't get far then.'

'No, a couple of miles at the most.'

'And Max?'

'No sign, I'm sorry.'

'Poor bugger.'

Crane wasn't sure if he meant Sgt Green or Max. 'Did you know anything about what Green was planning when he disappeared. Clearly whatever it was, got him in hot water. But it's Max I'm worried about. God knows where he is, or with whom. Is there anything you know that could help me?'

Crane was careful not to alienate the man by accusing him of doing either something, or nothing.

'Well, yes, possibly, but it was a secret.'

'What was?' Crane pushed.

'A school, a bursary place apparently. Green didn't want everyone knowing and taking up the places. It was a very limited intake apparently. He guarded it jealously. Hadn't even told Johanne. I kind of figured that's what had happened. And that he'd gone with Max.'

'Why didn't you tell anyone at the time?'

'Not my place, mate. It was Green's secret.'

'And you don't know the name of the school? Where it was? When Max was going?'

'No, sorry, mate.'

'Firstly,' said Crane. 'I'm not your bloody mate. And secondly, if you'd have bloody told someone at the time, then Max may have been traced and found. As it is he's disappeared down a black hole.'

'So you reckon he's still alive then?'

'I've no evidence to the contrary and until I do, I'll keep digging. We're talking about a vulnerable child here. I hope you can live with the consequences of you keeping shtum,' Crane hissed and abruptly turned away from Brown, before he'd do something he'd regret.

Chapter 9

As Crane returned to Provost Barracks, slamming through the door, still angry with Brown, Dudley-Jones called to him.

'What?' Crane demanded.

'Woah, who pulled your chain?'

'Bloody Sgt Brown. He knew something about Green's disappearance and didn't tell anyone.'

'What did he know?'

'That there was talk about a bursary place at a very well-respected school. When he and Max disappeared, he'd just assumed Green had gone with his son.'

'Bloody hell. Well, that ties in with what I've found.'

Crane raised an eyebrow.

'There's a text about a meeting, set for when we think Green was killed and Max was taken.'

'Excellent. So they could have met, with a place in a school as the bait,' said Crane.

'But it was a scam and Green was shot and the kid was taken.'

'Exactly, DJ. What sort of scam do you reckon?' Crane asked.

'It could be something that's being going on for years, particularly in poor countries when parents have too many children and they can't feed them. So, scammers offer to give their child a better chance in life, by a body of people supposed to be from, say a church or a charity. The trouble is the parents never see their child again, as they are sold to prospective adoptive parents.'

'That sounds awful,' Crane shuddered. 'Do you think it's true? About the school I mean?'

'I bloody well hope so,' said Dudley-Jones. 'Otherwise, the alternative doesn't bear thinking about.'

'Do you think he's on the Isle of Man then?'

'God only knows at the moment, but it's got to be worth checking out. Maybe there was some truth to their lies.' Dudley-Jones took a deep breath. 'Working on that premise, I've done some research.

'Yes?' Crane asked eagerly.

Dudley-Jones handed over a piece of paper. 'Here is a list of schools on the Isle of Man.'

'You've started there.'

'Well,' said Dudley-Jones, 'let's face it it's as good a place as any.'

But Max could be anywhere in the world, Crane thought. But decided to keep that to himself.

Sat at his desk, Crane racked his brains as to what else he could do. He aimlessly turned Green's phone over and over in his hands. What on earth could they do to try and find Max? If he was even alive. But Crane clung to the fact that they hadn't found any child's bones in that section of the canal. If he were honest with himself, he doubted Max had been killed. A beautiful boy would be a good asset to be sold to paedophiles or to childless couples as Dudley-Jones intimated. Either scenario made Crane shudder. He couldn't imagine Daniel being snatched from him and disappearing into a black hole never to be seen again. Crane's life would be over. Losing Tina and then Daniel would be too much to bear. No wonder Mrs Green had given up on life to all intents and purposes.

Then Crane had an idea. He turned on Green's mobile and took a note of the number that he'd got a message from, about meeting up. Firing up his laptop he typed the number into the search bar and pressed go.

As the hits began to appear, Crane saw a number of them also talked about missing children. Oh God, he thought, this could be bigger than he'd ever imagined. Needing caffeine before he faced the posts, he wandered into the kitchen, hands in his pockets. He stood looking out of the window at the sun shining down and shook his head at the wickedness in the world. Most people would never rub shoulders with this sort of evil and he envied their innocence. For he could well see a scenario where children were lured from their parents, with the draw being giving their offspring a better future.

Coffee made, Crane returned to his desk, took a deep breath

and began to read.

Chapter 10

What he found was truly awful. There was a Facebook group. Of course there was, Crane thought. There was a Facebook group for tying your shoelaces! Cynicism apart, he also knew that as frivolous as some of the groups could be, they did represent a lifeline to others. And parents of lost children needed some direction in life. Other people who understood what they were going through. Someone who would listen to their story.

It was all so heart wrenching.

I thought I was doing the right thing. Giving him a better start in life. For that's what education is, isn't it? A better start? Oh, what have I done…!

This bloke contacted me outside the food bank. They knew I had nothing. They knew my kid was growing up without new shoes, without clothes that fitted. Was going hungry. They said they were from a charity. They were so nice and kind. A man and a woman they were. They left me with a brochure and said to think about it. It's been four weeks now since he left. I've not had a phone call or message. I've tried constantly to get in touch with them, but the phone number doesn't work anymore. I've searched and searched for the name of the school online, but it doesn't seem to exist. I'm at my whit's end. What else should I do? Can anyone help? I'm going mad here!

Four weeks! Four weeks! It's been 4 years since Mikie went missing. Four long, horrible, empty, wasted years. I've nothing to live for now. My husband left, my son is missing, what's left for me? More years of misery? I can't take much more.

Thank God I found this group. Someone contacted me outside Poundsavers. It's the only shop I can afford. They said what a beautiful girl my Hollie was. Did she go to school? I told them yes, proudly telling them how intelligent she was. They said she deserved a bright future and that they could give her one. Their charity gave school bursaries, and they gave me a brochure. A man and a woman it was. What should I do?

Block their number! Tear up the brochure! Tell the police, but for goodness sake don't let Hollie go with them! They are a con, they're scum, they're worse than you can ever imagine. If you love your daughter keep her close. Don't let them take her!

Crane put his head in his hands. He couldn't read any more. Wished he had a cigarette, that he still smoked. Instead, he went outside to clear his head. He thought of all the times he'd stood outside Provost Barracks over the years, cigarette in hand, butts littering the floor. Of all the cases he'd dealt with, missing and dead children were the worst. And it looked like Crane had just opened a can of worms. He needed to try and contact some of these women. Take statements from them. Check with their local police force. It looked like Crane had stumbled upon a child abduction ring. Their objective not yet know, but Crane could only hope the children had been sold to adopting parents who couldn't have children of their own and would give a youngster a great life.

Maybe. Maybe not. Who knew?

Crane had to find out.

With renewed determination, he strode back indoors.

Chapter 11

Crane wrote Facebook messages to three of the women active in the group. Only one replied. The woman who had not handed over her child Hollie. Her name was Maddie and she agreed to a video call.

Crane made the call and sat for a while as Maddie got herself together.

'Thanks for speaking to me, Maddie,' he started.

She looked at him without saying anything.

'As I said, my name is Sgt Major Crane and I'm working on behalf of the Military Police from Provost Barracks in Aldershot.'

'How do I know that's true?' she said.

'Would you like to call the barracks?'

'Yes, I think that's a very good idea.'

'I do understand,' Crane said, although he was champing at the bit to get going. 'My phone number is…'

'I'll find it myself,' she said then the screen went blank.

Crane huffed and pushed his chair from his desk. It was understandable, after what she'd been through. He prowled the barracks, not knowing what else to do. He didn't want to tell anyone he was waiting for Maddie to call. She had to be convinced he was on the level.

He was loitering in reception, when he heard a young woman say, 'Yes, that's right, Sgt Major Crane does work here. Would you like to speak to him?'

Maddie must have said yes, as she handed the phone to him.

'Crane,' he said.

'So, you are real then.'

'Very much so.'

'OK, let's do that video call.'

'Thank you,' he said, but Maddie had already gone.

Nodding to the receptionist, he handed her back the phone and walked to his office, to find his laptop ringing.

'So, what do you want?' Maddie said as Crane answered, and

the video camera sprung into action.

'First of all, I was sorry to hear of your very upsetting incident.'

'Thank you, but at least I didn't fall for their claptrap, for that's what it was, wasn't it?'

'Rather more sinister than that, I'm afraid,' Crane said. 'To be honest, you've had a lucky escape.'

'I know,' Maddie said, 'but a part of me wanted it to be real, you know? To give Hollie a better start in life.'

'Yes, I understand, but how far would you go to achieve that?'

'Not to never see her again, that's not what I want. I love her so much and I'm determined to give her the best I can afford. Hollie is my only focus and the thought of not having her with me anymore ....' She gulped then continued, 'It doesn't bear thinking about.'

Crane could understand that. He felt exactly the same about Daniel. Clearing what felt like a rock in his throat, he said, 'Will you help me find them?'

'Of course, but how?'

'By giving me a statement about what happened.'

Maddie nodded. 'Ok,' she said in a small voice.

'I don't want to upset you.'

She sniffed then said, 'You couldn't make me more upset than I already feel, so let's do this.'

'Are you alright with me recording this call?' Crane had to make sure she understood. 'I might need to share this with other law enforcement officers and use it to help catch those responsible for all these children going missing.'

Maddie sat up squarely on her chair. 'Yes, of course, let's do this.'

Chapter 12

'My name is Sgt Major Tom Crane from Provost Barracks, Aldershot.'

Crane nodded at Maddie.

'My name is Madelaine Pew of 29 Lewis Road, Pembroke.'

'Now, I understand you were approached when leaving Poundsaver with Hollie.'

'Yes, that's right. We'd just done a bit of shopping and were ready to go home. As we left the shop, there was a couple stood outside, you know how there are. Normally it's people from a local church. Outreach they call it.'

'But it wasn't them.'

'No. Anyway, so this couple, they just seemed to start talking to me. And to Hollie. Chatting away as though we knew each other.'

'But you didn't?'

'Never seen them before in my life. They intimated they were from that Church who are normally there, but they wanted to talk to me about Hollie. I wondered why, but they just wittered on, saying how beautiful she was, how was she doing at school, did she enjoy it? You know, that sort of shit.'

Crane nodded.

'Then they said that they had a very exciting opportunity for the right child. A child such as Hollie who was so lovely and intelligent to boot! Flattering me, you know?'

Once more Crane nodded, not wanting to interrupt the flow of her story.

'They showed me a brochure. This school, it looked just like a stately home, you know? Then they started talking about bursaries and said that meant it wouldn't cost me a penny to send her there. It's what they did, apparently. Find children who needed a lucky break and give them the best future possible. At least that's what they said.'

'How did they know who you were?'

'Well, that's the thing. I don't think they did know who I was. I had to give them my name, phone number and email address. They told me to read the brochure and then they'd be in touch in a few days to talk about it further.'

'And how did you feel about that?'

'I don't know, I was flattered I suppose, but it was all a bit of a whirlwind. They both were talking at me, like some sort of comedy duo, but what they were saying wasn't funny. They were deadly serious and very passionate about what they called 'their calling'. To work with a charity doing such good work.'

'Did they seem like crusaders. You know, from a cult kind of thing?'

'Possibly, they seemed very sincere.'

'But of course, we now know they were con artists,' said Crane. 'So, what did they look like?'

'Best as I can remember, dark suits, neat and tidy and beige raincoats.'

That conjured up images of Mormon believers, going on a pilgrimage to take the word of the Lord to the masses and to try and recruit them to their church. It was possible that this was deliberate, of course. In real life it was doubtful they looked like that. A brilliant disguise.

'What about hair colour?'

'Um, let me see... dark hair for the man, and for the woman come to that.'

'And you never heard names?'

'No, not once.'

'Let's think about the man. Did he wear glasses?'

'No.'

'Have a beard or any other facial hair?'

'Nope.'

'Any other distinguishing features?'

'No, sorry, he was just, well, bland, I suppose, thinking back.'

'And the woman?'

'Same really. No glasses, no make up, no nail varnish or jewellery. Nothing stands out at all, I'm so sorry. The best I can do is the image of them being Mormon, or some such.'

'That's pretty good, Maddie, thanks a lot. Did they ever ring you?'

'Well, I blocked them, so I don't know. Oh, wait a minute, I got an email from them, I've just remembered. Hang on while I look.'

Crane waited until she accessed her emails on her mobile.

'Yes, here it is, shall I forward it to you?'

'Yes, please that's very helpful.'

Crane didn't hold out much hope of finding out where they'd emailed from, if this lot were as good as he thought they were, then there would be VPNs all over the place, but he didn't want to discourage Maddie.

After giving her his email address he thanked her profusely. 'And if you think of anything else at all, please phone, message or email me.'

'Yes, of course I will. Now I better go, Hollie's calling for me.'

'Of course, thanks Maddie,' and Crane disconnected the call.

He puffed out a breath and sat for a moment. Even though he was convinced that the dark suit and beige raincoats were a cover to disguise their real identities, it could give him just the starting point he needed.

Chapter 13

Crane read the email. It was pretty innocuous:

Hi Maddie,

Nice to meet you the other day. Do you remember me? We talked about Hollie and a possible bursary place at our wonderful school on the Isle of Man. Why not visit the website of Queen Beatrix's College, www.qbc.sch.im. That will give you a good overview of the boarding school and all that it can offer Hollie.

I'll be in touch soon.

A friend.

Obviously, the website didn't work anymore, despite Crane's best efforts, still it was worth talking to Dudley-Jones.

But Dudley-Jones wasn't any more positive than Crane.

'Sorry, Sir, but I just can't find anything,' he said, after much clicking on his keyboard and seeing absolutely sod all on his monitor.

'Dudley-Jones, stop calling me Sir. I'm no more over you than you're over me. My name is Crane. That's it. Just Crane.'

Dudley-Jones grinned, 'Whatever you say, Sir,' and ducked before Crane could ruffle his hair.

Turning away, Crane decided it was time he updated Billy, who was sat in his office, but with his door open. A closed door meant 'bugger off' an open one meant 'come in if you dare.' Another habit Billy had learned from Crane back in the day.

As Crane knocked on the door, Billy raised his head.

'Ah, Crane, come to update me?'

'Please, Billy, if you're free.'

'Of course, come in.'

Once settled in a seat, with his file in his hands, Crane told Billy of his interviews with Mrs Green and Sgt Green's mate, Sgt Brown.

'So, we're looking at some sort of scam.'

'Yes. We think they lure children from their parents, by offering bursary places.'

'And then the children are never seen again?'

'Exactly. This is the recurring theme. There's even a Facebook group about it.' Crane explained that he'd managed to interview one of its members, who had refused to send her daughter Hollie away.

'So where do we go from here?' asked Billy.

'Well, I'd like permission to brief DI Wood. It may help if the police can search their HOLMES system to look for other cases and other 'Mormon type' people contacting them or accosting them in the street.'

'Absolutely,' said Billy. 'Let's see what they can dig up. Thanks, Crane.'

Crane recognised a dismissal when he heard it and left.

Back at his desk, he rang Aldershot Police Station and was lucky enough to find DI Wood at his desk.

'Yes, Crane, what do you want now?'

Crane ignored the deliberately bored intonations in Wood's voice and succinctly told Wood why he was calling.

'Really?' the detective said, perking up. 'That's terrible!' Wood was clearly no longer bored.

'So,' Crane concluded, 'I'd like help from you to do searches on HOLMES and see if there are any other cases with similarities. Missing children, school bursaries, Mormon-type people reaching out to them. I'm afraid this is not something just local to Aldershot. It could well be happening in other parts of the UK.'

'Agreed,' said Wood without delay. 'I'll speak to Bevins, you've worked with him before, and he'll be in touch.'

'Quickly?'

'As soon as he's on duty.'

The conversation over, Crane relaxed. The next step in the enquiry had been taken. Crane hoped the outlook was positive but was very much afraid it wouldn't be. How many more children had suffered? How many more parents devastated? Crane almost didn't want to know but had to face it.

And so, he did the only thing he could. Left work and went home to Daniel.

He needed a hug.

Chapter 14

Once Bevins was on duty the following day, he rang Crane.

'Morning, Crane,' the Sergeant said. 'DI Wood told me to call you.'

'Did he tell you why?'

'Yes, child abduction. A kid called Max disappeared about four years ago. The father was the man we fished out of the Basingstoke Canal. But child abduction? Are you sure? Just the thought of it makes me shudder.'

'I know, but I've found a Facebook group for parents of children that have gone missing with the same criteria, and it seems as though this is a country wide thing, not just restricted to Aldershot.'

'Right.'

'Can you do a search on HOLMES, widen the search area to the whole of the UK, and cover the last four years. We're looking for anyone complaining of Mormons knocking on doors, children going missing with Mormons mentioned, scams about free places at schools.'

'All of them at once?' Bevins sounded sceptical.

Crane thought for a moment. 'No, you're right, that would be too confusing. Split the searches up into what you think will return the best results.'

'Right, I'll call you when I have some news.'

In the meantime, Crane did more searches on Facebook, Instagram and Tik Tock to see if he could find any more mention of scams involving children. He was in the middle of this task when Bevins rang again.

'You'll never believe this,' he started with. 'I did a search around Aldershot first, as that's where Max disappeared. There were reports of a couple like this around Aldershot at the time of Max's disappearance. Here's a mug shot.'

Crane's mobile pinged and he immediately opened the photograph. The man was just as Maddie had described. Nondescript.

'I'll send everything through on an email now.'

'Thanks, Bevins, I really appreciate this.'

'No worries. Let me know where we go from here.'

'Will do,' and Crane cleared the call, heartened by Bevins' use of the word, we.

Opening the email, the first thing Crane did was to print it off and the various attachments. Walking into the Cold Case Room, Crane laid the pages out on his table.

It seemed the main suspect, Andik Vata, was of Albanian heritage with links to organised crime, who also went by the name of Andy Varley.

Bevins had included details of the man himself and any known associates. According to the police, he was suspected of various nefarious crimes. More interestingly Bevans had included a list of people who had been duped by him through various scams, not just the boarding school one. It seemed Vata had been a very busy boy. However, there was no concrete evidence, so nothing the police could do without a confession, which they were clearly not going to get. But it seemed Vata was certainly active in the area when Max disappeared. Furthermore, his criminal record showed that he had been jailed on drug charges for three years in 2015, but only served two.

There were also reports that he had a female companion Loke Pllum, who also went by the name Lucy Plum. Once more, her mug shot showed a normal looking woman, devoid of make up or jewellery. Both Andik and Loke looked like British citizens and spoke without any accent, due to being born here of Albanian parents. Bevins had put out a call to Aldershot and other police forces, for anyone seeing either of them, to arrest them but proceed with caution.

Crane made a note to ask Max's mother about Mormons seen on the garrison.

Bevins was now widening the search area and covering the past four years. Anyone reporting children going missing, with Mormon's mentioned. Of course, if it was Andik and Loke they may not use the same ruse every time. But Crane figured if something worked and they'd perfected it, why change it?

If it ain't broke, don't fix it.

Chapter 15

Reading through the paperwork on Andik, Crane found that one of Andik's known associates, Adiim Hassan, was currently residing in Winchester Prison and Crane called Bevins.

'You know how I'm supposed to get support from the police and that you are my liaison,' Crane said.

'Yes,' said Bevins guardedly.

'I thought we'd go and have a little chat with Adiim in Winchester.'

'A little chat? Hang on, did you just say we?'

'Absolutely,' Crane said. 'It'll be a treat for you, getting out and about instead of being stuck indoors all day.'

'You're kidding me? With this weather?'

Crane looked out of the window. Rain was pounding down on the cars in the carpark. Bevins had a point, he had to concede. But he wasn't to be deterred.

'Go on, Bevins, give Winchester a ring and arrange for us to go today. The rain will probably have stopped by then.'

Grinning, Crane cut the call before Bevins could object.

It was later that day that Crane and Bevins arrived at Winchester Prison. Crane was right the rain had stopped and the sun was peeking through holes in the cloud. Once at the prison they had to hand in their belongings and were only allowed to take in their files and a recorder to record the interview, into the room. They only had a few minutes to wait before Adiim was brought in.

Crane looked the man up and down. Basically, a thug. He'd met enough of them in the army not to be intimidated by the man's bulk and attitude. Adiim sat down astride a chair which was bolted to the floor, legs open in a typical man-spread pose, cracking his knuckles for effect. Crane almost laughed, but Bevins kicked his ankle to sober him up.

Bevins led the interview.

'Morning, Adiim,' Bevins started. 'My name is Sgt Bevins

from Aldershot Police and this here is Sgt Major Crane from Provost Barracks, on Aldershot Garrison.'

'So?' Adiim shrugged.

'So we have an investigation which we'd like your input on.'

'Input?' the man's brows knitted together. His thick accent discernible from just those two words. To Crane's ear it sounded Russian.

'We have a historical case of possible child abduction we wondered if you'd be able to help us with.'

'Me? Help the pigs?' Adiim laughed. 'Now why the hell would I do that?'

'Because I've had a word with the Governor, and he's willing to give you enhanced privileges in return.'

'Is he now?' Adiim's eyebrows raised.

'Absolutely. Interested now?' said Crane. 'That means extra money, more time outdoors and a tv in your cell.'

'I know what it means,' Bevins growled.

'So, are you interested?'

'I might be. Tell me what you want to know first.'

Bevins told Adiim about the case they were working on. 'We're trying to bring Max home,' he finished with. 'So do you know of any child abduction scams the Albanian Maffia were running in the UK? We don't need names, but an idea of what the end game was. Where would the children go?'

'Please, Adiim, it's very important and you wouldn't be ratting anyone out. Look, you're a father yourself. Think about how you'd feel if it was your child being abducted,' Crane said.

'I'd tear the men who did it, limb from limb,' Adiim roared, and Crane knew he'd touched a nerve.

'So, help us. Help other parents find their lost children.'

'And no names?'

'Definitely no names,' confirmed Bevins.

After a few moments' silence, Adiim looked at each man in turn, then gave a sharp nod of his head. 'But you never say where this information came from.'

'Never,' agreed Bevins.

'Never,' confirmed Crane.

'Very well. I know of one operation where children would be snatched on the pretext of sending them to a posh boarding school and then sell them to childless couples.'

'Were the schools in the UK? Or was that where the couples were?'

'No, the children were taken only to the Isle of Man, Jersey and Guernsey. Prospective parents had to meet us there. I don't know if they lived there and frankly I don't care.'

'So why those islands?'

'Because they're crown dependencies. Less scrutiny than here on the mainland. And you don't need a passport to travel there.'

'And the children really were placed with adoptive parents?'

'Sure, at £10,000 a kid, we, I mean they, made a lot of money.'

'But how did you get away with it?'

'The childless couples said they'd adopted legally and were supplied with forged papers. The children were young enough to forget their actual parents and accept their adopted ones without question.'

'Did all the childless couples live in the Crown Dependencies?'

'No, some of them went over for holidays and returned with a child. No passport control, no nothing. Roll on roll off ferries, you understand?'

Crane slumped in his chair. It had been that easy.

Chapter 16

Driving back to Aldershot, Crane got Bevins to do a search on the Isle of Man. He knew nothing about it, had never visited, equally the Channel Islands, but they'd start with the Isle of Man for now as that's where Max was supposedly been going to school.

Bevins read, 'The Isle of Man is a self-governing British Crown dependency in the Irish Sea between England and Ireland. It's known for its rugged coastline, medieval castles and rural landscape, rising to a mountainous centre. In the capital, Douglas, the Manx Museum traces the island's Celtic and Viking heritage. The Isle of Man TT is a major annual motorcycle race around the island.'

'So that's the Isle of Man,' Crane said. 'I'd never even given it a second thought. Neither Jersey nor Guernsey. You?'

'Nah, if I go on holiday, it's to the Costas. The wife likes her holiday on sunbeds on the beach or around the pool, then a few drinks and dinner of a night. Simple pleasures.'

Crane smiled. 'Indeed Bevins. A lot more restful than taking Daniel to Disneyland Paris, which is what I'm doing in the summer holidays.'

'Ha, ha,' laughed Bevins. 'Rather you than me. You'll need a holiday to get over your holiday! But what's our next move?'

Crane like the use of the word, our. 'I need to get publicity on the Islands. See if anyone has seen Max Green, or if anyone else knows of this adoption scam. If I draft something up, can you pass it to the police please? I'll get in touch with the local press on the Isle of Man and the Channel Islands, actually probably through Diane Chambers, and get a piece put in the Aldershot News as well. You never know, someone else might have been approached before they settled on Max.'

Crane figured it was easier to go to Diane Chambers than have her on the Garrison, so after dropping Bevans off, he parked on the High Street and walked to the paper's offices, which were situated above an estate agent. As he walked in a receptionist greeted him.

'Good afternoon, how can I help you?'

'Is Diane in please?'

'Yes, but I'm not sure if she's free.'

'Trust me, she will be, tell her it's Sgt Major Crane.'

Just then a door behind reception opened. 'I heard that, Crane. This is very unexpected, walking into the lion's den,' she grinned. 'Sally, get us two coffees would you? One black one white, no sugar and bring them through. Come on, Crane, if you're brave enough.'

As they walked through the newsroom Crane noticed that it was very quiet compared to how it used to be back in the day. 'Low on staff these days, are you?' he said as they entered Diane's messy office.

She moved a pile of newspapers so he could sit down.

'So much is done online now, Crane,' she said. 'Most of them work from home now.'

'But not you?'

'No, old school, me.'

Crane grinned. 'You and me both.'

Just then Sally came in, handing Crane a black coffee and Diane a white.

Once she'd left, Diane said, 'So, Crane, I'm sure you're not here to catch up on old times. What do you want?'

'Publicity for a cold case I'm working. Remember the skeleton that was found in the Basingstoke canal?'

Diane nodded.

'Well he's been identified and his child, Max is missing.'

That made her lean forward with interest. 'Go on,' she said. 'Oh, do you mind if I record this conversation?'

'I'm surprised you even asked,' he said, raising an eyebrow.

'Well, I am the Editor now and I have to play by the rules,' she said as she placed her mobile phone on the desk between them and set it to record.

Crane didn't need any further encouragement and he told her everything they knew about the case.

'Bloody hell that's horrible,' she said with a shudder. 'Fancy losing a child like that!'

'I know, so what I need from you is publicity. Firstly, here in Aldershot, but can you also get the papers on the Isle of Man, Jersey and Guernsey interested and get them to do a piece. To start with let's focus on Max Green, to see if we can trace him first. Can you ask anyone who thinks they've seen him to contact Bevins at Aldershot Police.'

'Not you?'

'No, I must play by the rules too. I don't have any jurisdiction anywhere. Bevins is my police liaison, direct them to him.' Crane stood. 'Thanks for this, Diane. I really need your help.'

'My pleasure, now let me get on with it. I'll send you a copy of the article.'

Crane nodded his head and left the office, feeling more positive than he had been when he arrived.

Chapter 17

Goodwin Slater entered his private study with a swish of his academic robes. A tall, thin man with balding grey hair, he towered over the boys in the school of which he was Headmaster. He knew he was old school. Revelled in the values and behaviour of a world long gone, where manners counted for everything and everyone was expected to do their best, without question. Personal hygiene was paramount and clothes needed to be looked after, as did their bedrooms.

But sometimes the work got the better of him. Running a school of 30 staff and 300 boys on the Isle of Man, wasn't easy and on a Friday night he often felt his age. Pouring himself a stiff whisky, he sat at his desk with a sigh and pulled the local paper towards him. He'd just have a short relaxing break before dinner, but the headline on the front page brought a frown to his face. *Has a child abduction ring been working on the Isle of Man?*

Child abduction? The Isle of Man? It didn't compute. Scratching his bald patch he began to read:

It all began with the discovery of bones found in the Basingstoke Canal in Aldershot. Some way away readers might think. But read on, all will be revealed.

What was this? Some sort of murder mystery, thought Goodwin? Yet he continued to read, being dragged into the article.

The victim turned out to be a Sgt Green who had gone missing from Aldershot Garrison at the same time as his four year old son, some five years ago. For years it was thought that Sgt Green had disappeared with his son, Max, as his marriage was breaking down and he wanted custody of the child. But now it appears that theory was just a load of speculation. However, it has raised many more questions. How come Green was in the Basingstoke Canal? We know he was killed, as his skull had a neat hole in it in the forehead. So, he was murdered. But why? And where is Max?

Aldershot Police and the Military Police joined forces and have uncovered a ring of Albanian criminals who abducted small children and then sold them into adoption to childless couples who were desperate for a child. If they could pay £10,000 then they got a kid. It's not known if children were abducted to order or if the gang were more opportunistic.

Naive parents down on their luck, or without any money to give their child a better future were targeted, with the lure of a fancy boarding school where their children would want for nothing and be educated to a very high standard. The schools were described as being in Jersey, Guernsey or the Isle of Man.

A shiver ran down Goodwin's back. That was about the time that Strickland, one of the teachers, joined the school.

Goodwin read on:

But, of course, the parents never saw their children again.

The police are looking for Max Green, now missing for nearly five years. The pictures depict Max at four (the last photograph his mother has of him) and an artist's impression as to how Max could look now.

His mother has made this impassioned plea. 'If you have Max, or you have any suspicions at all that a child you know could be my son, then please get in touch with your local police. Max was my world and I'm desperate to have him back. I've lost everything I held dear and can't hold on for much longer. Please help me.'

The blood drained from Goodwin's face. It couldn't be, could it? But the age fitted. The dates fitted. The photographs fitted. With much trepidation Goodwin reached for a personnel file which he kept locked in his desk. Flicking through it he confirmed the dates and ages, then picked up the phone.

Chapter 18

Sgt Bevins was once more on duty at the front desk of Aldershot Police Station, and he was bored. He had to grudgingly admit that he enjoyed being out and about with Crane, doing some proper police work. Okay so he'd been a bit grumpy when told by DI Woods that he was to help the Military Police, but now he was a convert. But they were waiting for something to happen into the investigation of lost Max Green and so he was back as Desk Sergeant.

The phone ringing broke his introspection. 'Bevins,' he said.

'Sarge there's a call for you from some bloke on the Isle of Man. Says he knows where Max Green is.'

Immediately his pulse jumped. 'You better put him through,' he said, trying for calm and failing. 'Sgt Bevins, how can I help you.'

'I think I know where Max Green is. Although he's not called that anymore. Anyway, you have to come, it could be him. I got your details from ringing the Manx police and they said to contact you directly.'

Bevins relied on his training and said, 'First things first, Sir, can you give me your name and location?'

'What? Oh yes, sorry. Goodwin Slater, I'm Headmaster at King Edward international school on the Isle of Man.

'And the address and phone number?'

Slater gave them.

'Thank you, Mr Slater, now you think you know Max Green?'

'Yes, but he's known as Jeremy Strickland here'

'Is he a pupil?'

'Yes. Um yes, his father is a teacher here.'

'And the father's name?'

'George Strickland. His wife is called Mavis and they live in a cottage in the grounds. Staff cottage you understand. And Jeremy comes to school here for free. Being the son of staff.'

'Very well. And why do you think this lad could be our

missing Max Green?'

'Well, he looks like the photographs published in the paper.'

'Right. Anything else?'

'His parents arrived nearly five years ago with a child I knew nothing about.'

'Nothing?'

'No, it wasn't on George's application for the post, nor mentioned during the zoom call interview. He had excellent references and so I took him on immediately. But when he arrived, he had a son with him, and he said sorry he'd forgotten to mention it. Well, there was nothing I could do but to allow him into school. I urgently needed a teacher so I didn't want to send him away, but I wasn't happy as you can imagine.'

'Quite.'

'Anyway, it was rather strange. When the boy first arrived, I'd call him by his name, and he wouldn't react. It was as if he thought I were talking to someone else when I called him Strickland. He didn't seem to register that that was his name. Well obviously, that wore off, but it did strike me as very bloody strange at the time.'

'Are there any plans for the Stricklands to move from the school?'

'No, not that I'm aware of.'

'Very well. I'll come over to the Isle of Man with my colleague Sgt Major Crane. I don't want you to say anything to anyone about this, do you understand?'

'Yes, yes of course.'

'In the meantime, please send me a picture of the Strickland boy, would you? Could you do that on WhatsApp?'

'Yes, yes, of course.'

'Send it directly to my mobile. Here's the number,' and Bevins read it out and had Goodwin Slater read it back to him.

'Thank you, Headmaster. It was very good of you to call. I'll call you tomorrow with our travel arrangements. Is there a best time to get in touch with you?'

'Yes, I'm in my study between 12 pm and 2 pm every day,

dealing with the administration of the school, you can reach me then.'

'Thank you, we'll speak tomorrow,' and Bevins replaced the receiver with a shaking hand.

Was it really possible they'd found Max Green? Or would they be going to the Isle of Man on a wild goose chase?

Chapter 19

Mavis Strickland couldn't shake the disquiet she was feeling. It had started with Jeremy having those nightmares, or night terrors, or whatever the hell they were. And now the Headmaster had started to give them funny looks. At least Mavis thought he had. George on the other hand thought it was all in her head. She was obsessing about something that was nothing and therefore wasn't worth worrying about. He was dismissing her disquiet out of hand. But Mavis could feel something in her bones. And that something was fear.

Where had Jeremy actually come from? Why was he talking about tanks and guns? Had he come from a war zone? If so then he could be psychologically damaged and need specialist help. George thought Jeremy would grow out of the nightmares, but what if he didn't? She'd tried to tackle George about Jeremy's background, but he said that just wasn't relevant. All she needed to know was that she was so desperate to have a child, she would have done anything.

At the time adoption had seemed an easy way to become parents, but they'd been turned down by the agencies that ran the schemes. They were too old, apparently, for a baby or young child. Mavis' devastation had been complete. She'd lost interest in everyone and everything and took herself off to bed and refused to get up.

That's when George said he'd take matters into his own hands. She had no idea what that meant, but one day George returned home from school and asked her to come downstairs. She'd grudgingly agreed, but had refused to change out of her old, smelly pyjamas, which let's face it went with her long, dirty, greasy hair. He'd asked her to follow him into the kitchen, where he sat her down and gave her a mug of coffee.

'We're moving,' he'd said.

'What? What are you talking about?'

'I've got a new job and we're going to the Isle of Man.'

'The Isle of where?'

'Man. It's in the Irish Sea.'

'Why on earth are we doing that?'

'Because once there, we can adopt a child.'

Mavis was stunned. 'Adopt? A child?'

'Yes, my dear,' Geroge had said. 'A boy. A son. We can adopt him. He's four years old, comes from a harsh background and needs a welcoming loving home.'

Mavis was lost for words. 'But how? Why? When?'

'You missed it all being depressed and in bed,' George had said. 'So, I had to make a decision on my own. Did I do good?' he grinned at her.

She smiled. The first one in a long time. 'Yes, you did good, George.'

'Would you like to help me pack?'

Mavis looked down at her filthy pyjamas. 'Not yet, I think I should shower and wash my hair first.'

'Excellent idea, love. I'll get some boxes out of the garage.'

And that had been over four years ago. George and Mavis had moved within the week to the Isle of Man, where Jeremy appeared. George had arranged everything without telling her. It was as though Mavis had a hole in her life, with days, weeks and months missing. She knew now she'd had a breakdown and that George had done everything on his own, all with the intention of pulling her out of her malaise. And it had worked.

Jeremy had settled in well. They'd never talked about his past, just let it die a natural death. Not once did he ever talk about previous parents, or where he'd lived before. Instead, they'd moved forward as a family.

But now Mavis felt as though the strong foundations of the life they'd built on the Isle of Man were crumbling beneath her feet and depression was once more gathering like storm clouds in the back of her mind.

Chapter 20

Crane was at home on Sunday when a WhatsApp message arrived, from Bevins of all people. It was a photograph of a young boy, and the message underneath was, 'Ring me.'

Intrigued, Crane did just that, leaving Daniel to continue watching the film on his own and going to the kitchen, taking a seat at the kitchen table.

It didn't take long for Bevins to fill Crane in and by that time Crane was prowling around the kitchen. 'Do you think he's genuine?' Crane asked.

'Well, I did some digging before I called you and there is a King Edward international school on the Isle of Man and the Headmaster is Goodwin Slater. So, he does seem to be on the level. I can't find out if there is a Jeremy Strickland at the school but one of the teachers is indeed George Strickland. There's talk of staff cottages and also free places for the children of staff. So yes, I think he's on the level. Is the boy our Max Green? Well that's another matter.'

'So, can we go? To the Isle of Man?'

'Yes, DI Wood has authorised us to go to pursue the investigation. There are flights from Gatwick. Can you go tomorrow?'

'Yes, that's fine with me. Daniel will be alright with the au pair who is back on duty tomorrow morning.'

'Great, I'll get the flights booked and text you. I'll get a car to take us to the airport. Bring an overnight bag just in case.'

'Will do, Bevins. And thank you.'

'No need for thanks, Crane. Just doing my job. And I want to find this boy as much as you do. See you tomorrow.'

When Crane got back to the living room, the film was just finishing.

'You missed the ending, Dad!'

'Yes, sorry, son.'

'Was it work?'

Crane nodded.

'Are you going out now, then?'

Crane smiled. 'No, not tonight, but I'll be going to the Isle of Man tomorrow. On an aeroplane!'

'Wow! Um, what's the Isle of Man?'

Crane grinned. 'Come on, let's get your tablet out and look it up, shall we, before bed? Then you'll know exactly where I am tomorrow. Deal?'

But there was no reply as Daniel was already rummaging for his tablet.

Chapter 21

The next morning, Crane was pleased to see that Bevins was out of uniform. The last thing they wanted to do was to spook the Stricklands before they'd had a chance to talk to them. A police car got them swiftly to Gatwick and they were soon on the plane. Being police on an active case seemed to give them priority and they were first on the plane and first off. When they arrived, on the tarmac was an unmarked car from the Manx police.

'What service!' said Crane. 'I'm not used to this I must say.'

'Well don't get used to it,' Bevins replied. 'It's only because we're on a case and there is a minor involved. Anyway, enjoy it while you can.'

They were whisked away from the airport and very soon after that, King Edward international school came into view.

Crane whistled. 'Bloody hell. It's even more imposing than the website!'

'So, you looked it up then.'

'Of course I did, once Daniel had gone to bed. You were right about everything checking out. The Headmaster and the Stricklands.'

'Yes, well, we're incognito for now. Let's start with the Headmaster, Goodwin Slater.'

The car stopped in front of the main entrance of the school. 'Shall I wait for you?' the driver asked?

'No, you're alright. I guess you're never far away on the Island.'

The policeman grinned. 'No. I'll go back to headquarters so ring me when you've finished.'

'I might be ringing you when we've just started,' Bevins said enigmatically. 'Here, put your number in my phone and I'll call you.'

'Will do, Guv.'

Once that was done, Bevins and Crane climbed the steps to the front of the school. A large wooden door barred their way. It reminded Crane of the type found on churches. Crane turned the round handle, but nothing happened.

'Here, there's an intercom,' Bevins said, pushing the button.

It was answered quickly. 'King Edward international school, how can I help you?'

'We are here to see Mr Slater, he's expecting us. Bevins and Crane.'

'Very well, come in. Someone will meet you in the hall.

With a loud buzz the front door unlocked. Crane pushed the door, which opened this time. As they walked in, they heard a clack clack of shoes from their left and into view came a smartly dressed woman in her 30's Crane guessed, with a shiny chestnut brown bob which swung as she walked.

'Mr Bevins, Mr Crane,' she said. 'If you'll follow me. Please don't use your rank, we don't want to alarm the children.'

'No, of course,' said Crane, hurrying to keep up with her. He'd been studying the hallway, which was enormous, with a large staircase sweeping up to upper floors. There were exposed beams on the ceiling and on the walls were wooden plaques with the names of boys on them, for various sports including rugby and cricket. 'And you are?' he asked.

'The Headmaster's assistant. Here we are...' and she stopped suddenly at a nondescript office door, which she opened and walked inside.

Crane and Bevins followed her into a modern office, which was no doubt hers as she walked to a second door, marked 'Headmaster' and opened it.

'Crane and Bevins, Sir,' she said and ushered them inside.

A man in academic robes was fussing over a coffee machine. 'Coffee?' he asked, holding a glass jug full of black liquid.

'Please,' said Crane. 'Black no sugar for me and white no sugar for Bevins here.'

Once they were seated with their coffees, Slater walked around his desk and sat down.

'Thank you for coming so quickly,' he said. 'This, um, situation is all I can think about, and I'm terrified of doing the wrong thing. What if it is your lost boy? But what if it isn't and I've made a terrible mistake?'

Chapter 22

To be fair, Crane didn't think Strickland had made a mistake. The key was that the dates fitted exactly from when Max and his father went missing, to arriving at the school the next day. It was just too suspicious to not interview the Stricklands.

But before they did that, Crane wanted to see Max Green, or Jeremy Strickland as he now was.

'I suggest we just see him while he's in class,' said Slater. 'I'm not sure calling him out would be a good idea.'

As Crane and Bevins demurred to that, he picked up the phone and said, 'Julie, where is Jeremy Strickland?'

'Right now?'

'Yes, right now.'

There was a clacking of keys and then she said, 'In the hall doing gymnastics.'

'Thank you,' he said and replaced the receiver. 'Shall we go for a walk?'

Slater led the way deeper into the school. All the corridors seemed like a rabbit warren and Crane soon lost his sense of direction. Everywhere was cream walls and wooden floors, mostly scuffed from thousands of pairs of feet with chunks taken out of the walls, no doubt from things being moved around the school. It all seemed a bit seedy, if Crane were honest. But he guessed that's what parents liked. The authenticity of it all. Schools that still looked as though they were in the Dickensian era.

'We have 300 boys,' the Headmaster explained as they walked, 'from Reception class all the way to 13, when the boys transfer to Eton or some such school. We take boarders from the age of 8 and they are mostly from parents who travel the world, or are Ministers of State, foreign dignitaries and the like. We have a capacity of 200 boarders, not an insubstantial number.'

Crane wondered what the fees were, eye watering no doubt. As they passed classrooms, he noted that all the teachers wore academic robes. Until they came to the hall. There a man with impressive arm muscles was dressed in a tee-shirt and joggers, with a whistle around his neck. Various equipment was laid out, from balance beams, to a pommel horse, climbing frames and ropes. The children appeared to be working their way around the room. They were dressed in shorts and singlets and most looked happy and slightly sweaty.

Goodwin Slater pointed out Jeremy Strickland who was sat next to the teacher, nursing his ankle. Leaving Crane and Bevins behind, Slater wandered over to the teacher. 'Good morning, Mr Ryan, sorry to disturb you, I'm just showing prospective parents around the school.'

Ryan didn't seem very chatty as he merely nodded to the Headmaster, his focus still on the children.

'What's the matter with you, Strickland?' Slater asked the boy.

'Turned my ankle, Sir,' Jeremy said.

'Does it hurt much?'

'Not too bad. Mr Ryan said to sit out for the rest of the class. It should be alright after that.'

'Very well.' The Headmaster looked at his watch. 'Not long before break,' he said. 'If it still hurts go and see Matron then.'

'Yes, Sir, thank you, Sir.'

Crane had been focusing on Jeremy Strickland and comparing him to the picture on his phone, which was in his hand. The Headmaster was right, he had a striking resemblance to Max Green. That was enough for Crane. He raised his eyebrows at Bevins, who nodded his agreement. When the Headmaster returned, they left the hall.

'I think you're right, Headmaster,' said Crane. 'At least a good enough match to have a word with the Stricklands.'

'Very well, let's go and see Mrs Strickland and I'll call George out of class and have him meet us there.'

Slater sent a message on his mobile, then turned to Crane and Bevins and said, This way,' leading them out of the back of the school, which was just as impressive in its own way, with acres of rolling green with large trees dotted around. A short way from the main school building, stood a cluster of cottages.

'Over there,' pointed Slater. 'Come on, I'll show you the Strickland's cottage,' and he strode off along a path running around the outside of the gardens.

As they approached the cottages Crane said, 'How do you want to play this, Bevins?' Turning to the Headmaster, he explained, 'Sgt Bevins here is police. I'm with the military police, but don't have any jurisdiction, that's why Bevins must lead the interview.'

'The Manx police know we're here and why,' explained Bevins. 'But for the moment we're just here to see if there could be any chance that Jeremy is our missing child.'

'Very well. Shall we go in, or wait for George?'

'Oh, go in, I think. I'd like to catch Mrs Strickland unaware.'

Slater nodded his head and rang the bell of a double fronted cottage, with pale green window frames and a matching front door.

A woman answered, wiping her hands on an apron. 'Oh, morning, Headmaster,' she said. Then spying Crane and Bevins added, 'What's wrong? What's happening? Where's George?'

'It's alright, Mavis,' said Slater. 'This is Sgt Major Crane and Sgt Bevins. They'd like to talk to you about Jeremy. Can we come in?' and Slater smoothly walked past Mrs Strickland, so Crane and Bevins followed him into a large, sunny kitchen, with Mrs Strickland trailing along behind.

'What's happening? Is Jeremy alright?' Mavis looked at each man in turn.

'Oh, yes, we're just wondering about Jeremy's parentage,' said Bevins, bluntly.

'I beg your pardon,' stammered Mavis. 'We are his parents.'

'Yes, but is he your biological son, or your adopted son?' Bevins wasn't giving any quarter.

'Oh,' Mavis fell into a chair and Crane hurried to get her some water as the woman had gone very pale.

'Thank you,' she said as he put a cup in her hands. Then she whispered, 'Adopted.'

'That's what we thought,' said Bevins and sat at the kitchen table next to her, with Crane and Slater joining him.

'When was he adopted and where from?' Bevins asked.

'What the hell is going on here?' George Strickland bellowed, making Mavis jump and drop the cup on the stone floor. 'Who are you to question my wife? Our son has nothing to do with you!'

Goodwin Slater stood. 'George, sit down, please. Look you're upsetting Mavis,' who indeed had begun sobbing into her apron.

From the oven came a strong burning smell, so Crane quickly stood, grabbed a tea towel and opened the door, removing a tray of burned biscuits. He placed the tray on the draining board and turned off the oven.

That seemed to have given George time to calm down and into the silence Bevins said, 'Mr Strickland, I'm Sgt Bevins of the Aldershot Police and this here is Sgt Major Crane from Aldershot Garrison. We understand that Jeremy is adopted.'

'That's correct,' blustered George. 'Not that it's any of your business.'

'That's where you're wrong, Sir,' said Bevins. 'Could we see your adoption papers?'

'Can they do this, Headmaster? We've done nothing wrong,' said Mavis.

'If you've done nothing wrong, nor have anything to hide, then what's wrong with showing them the paperwork?' Slater said smoothly.

'George?' asked Mavis.

But George didn't appear to be listening. He was holding his left arm and gasping. Sweat had broken out on his brow and as they watched, he tumbled off the chair and fell onto the floor.

'Quick, call an ambulance. He's having a heart attack,' said Crane who rushed to lay George out on the floor and place a towel under his head.

'It's his angina,' said Mavis. 'He should have tablets in his jacket pocket.'

Crane felt around George's jacket before finding a small tub in his top pocket. Shaking out a tablet he put it in George's mouth, under his tongue. Within a few minutes George was well enough to get off the floor and sit in a chair. But he was no longer angry. More resigned to the situation, than anything else.

'The adoption papers are in the bureau,' he said to Mavis. 'But they're forged.'

Mavis gasped. Crane was stunned. Could it possibly be that easy?

'I'm not going to make this worse for any of us. I'm sorry love, but I paid a man £10,000 for Jeremy. It's something I've had to live with for four long years. I knew it wasn't right. But we were desperate. You were so ill with depression. I didn't know how else to reach you.'

'So you planned it all?' asked Bevins. 'Without Mavis knowing?'

'Yes. I'm so sorry, love, but I did it all with the best of intentions.'

It was at that point that Mavis started to wail. Crane felt immensely sorry for the woman as no doubt she had just seen her happy family life disintegrate.

Chapter 23

Bevins took charge. 'Can we have the paperwork that you were supplied with please, Sir?' he asked George.

George nodded, then went to the bureau, situated in the corner of the dining part of the kitchen and rummaged through papers. As he was doing that, Bevins rang the Manx police, leaving the kitchen to go and make the arrangements.

George handed the certificate to Crane who examined the paperwork. It was a flowery certificate printed on stiff paper. It was all very lovely, but completely wrong.

'A Certificate of Adoption looks remarkably similar to a Birth Certificate,' said Crane. 'But says at the bottom left hand side that it is a *Certified copy of an entry made into the Adopted Children Register at the General Register Office.* Did you not know the real procedure? That it can take months? And that you have to go to Court?'

'Yes,' said George.

Mavis merely nodded her head.

'Mavis?' George looked astonished.

'I'd thought of that when Jeremy arrived but was too afraid to ask. I just knew that by some miracle we had a child and were moving to the Isle of Man to live in a pretty cottage in the school grounds, where you had a new job and Jeremy would go to school,' said Mavis.

'You can't have been that naive surely?' said Crane.

'No, not naive. Rather I didn't want to ask a question to which I was afraid of the answer.'

'So, you buried your head in the sand?'

'Yes, if you want to put it that way. Is that a crime?'

'I'm afraid so, Mrs Strickland,' said Bevins, returning to the kitchen. 'The Isle of Man police are on their way to arrest you both.'

'And Jeremy?' Mavis said weakly.

'He'll be taken to emergency foster parents no doubt and

as soon as his identify is confirmed through DNA, he'll come to Aldershot to be returned to his mother.'

'Can we see him before we go?'

'I'm afraid not,' said Bevins.

'But that's just cruel! Why can't we explain to him or say goodbye? George! Do something!'

'One moment please,' Crane pulled Bevins away and whispered. 'Is that strictly necessary? Can't you let them say goodbye?'

'I'm not supposed to. They're under arrest.'

'Yes, but not by the Manx police just yet. Think of what this will do to the boy! He'll have to live with this for the rest of his life. At least let him hear it from the people he thinks of as his parents. If you just pluck him out of school now and he doesn't really understand and he never sees George and Mavis again, that will affect him even more.'

'Well…'

'God, if anything awful happened to me and I was arrested, I couldn't imagine not being able to see Daniel one last time and let him know how loved he was and how sorry I was.'

'Well…'

The Headmaster walked over, 'Look poor Mavis is losing it completely. Please can't they just see him for a few minutes?'

'Oh, very well,' Bevins relented under the pressure from Crane and Slater.

Crane touched Bevins on the shoulder and squeezed his thanks. The Headmaster pulled his mobile out of his pocket and rang the ever efficient Julie.

It was merely five minutes later that Jeremy ran into the room. Following on was a woman the Headmaster introduced as Matron.

'I thought it would be a good idea to have Matron here. She'll be able to look after Jeremy. I was thinking that perhaps we could let him stay here as a boarder, you know, keep him in familiar surroundings. I am happy to act as a supervising adult, of course. And so will my wife and Matron.'

Bevins nodded. 'I'll see what I can do.'

'Mum, Dad,' they heard Jeremy shout. 'What's going on? What's the matter? Are you alright, Mum?'

They watched as George asked Jeremy to sit down and the three of them huddled together at the end of the kitchen table. George took one of Jeremy's hands and Mavis the other.

'Jeremy,' George said. 'We've something to tell you. Firstly, that you are adopted.'

'Adopted? Are you sure? You've never mentioned it before!'

'No, I know and that was probably a failing on my behalf,' said Geroge.

'We didn't want to upset you,' added Mavis.

'And there's something else,' George said.

Crane saw that Jeremy was looking like a startled rabbit caught in headlights.

'W w what else?'

Meanwhile Mavis was clearly trying hard not to sob.

'Your mum, I mean your real mum, didn't know about the adoption.'

'Didn't know? What on earth do you mean?'

'You were abducted,' Mavis said. 'And brought to us so we could adopt you.'

'Abducted? I don't understand.'

'We're so sorry, son, we love you so much and we did what we did out of love.'

Max was now crying as hard as Mavis and Crane was having difficulty holding onto his emotions. Then the sound of a car could be heard pulling up on the gravel drive outside.

'We have to go with the police, son,' said George.

'So we need to say goodbye,' said Mavis.

'We're so sorry,' George said, as he pulled Jeremy roughly towards him for a hug. Passing the boy to Mavis, he stood, cleared his voice and said, 'Very well, Sgt, let's go. Shall we meet the police outside?'

'That would be a good choice, Sir. Mrs Strickland, please, come with us.'

'Mum, no!' shouted Max.

'It's alright, Max,' said Matron. 'Let's go to your bedroom for a little bit, shall we?' and she led a distraught Jeremy out of the room.

Crane fell into a chair, feeling completely wrung out. He was convinced that the older he got the more emotional he became. He guessed it was what with Tina gone and being a single parent to a boy pretty much Jeremy's age. He could hear Bevins outside making arrangements with the Manx police and the soft sobbing of Mavis Strickland, echoed by that of her son inside the house.

Bevins returned. 'I've arranged that Jeremy can go with the Headmaster and Matron and we'll accompany them back to the school. Then we're to go to the police station and give formal statements.

Crane nodded, resigned to a long day, glad that they'd already arranged to stay over at a hotel in Douglas.

Chapter 24

'Max Green has had two lives,' Crane's statement began and went on to tell the Manx police about the first part of Max Green's life. He talked about the recent discovery of Sgt Green's remains in the Basingstoke Canal, near Aldershot and then detailed his investigation from that point forward. Finally he talked about Max's mother back in Aldershot.

By the time he'd finished, Crane was exhausted. After checking into the hotel, the first thing he did was to have a facetime call with Daniel.

'I'm sorry I'm not home, buddy,' he told his son. 'But I'll be back in a couple of days.'

'Oh,' Daniel's face fell. 'Are you still working?'

'I'm afraid so. I'm helping another boy, just a bit older than yourself, so it's really important that I stay.'

'That's alright, Dad.' Daniel managed a watery smile. Then cheered greatly and said, 'I've got James over and we have to finish this PlayStation game before his mum comes and collects him. So, I've got to go, Dad, bye!'

Crane smiled at the resilience of children as he finished the call with Marie Louise, the au pair, explaining that he'd be back as soon as he could.

'That's alright, Mr Tom,' she said. 'Daniel and I will be fine. I'll look after him.'

Greatly reassured that all was well at home, Crane went down to meet Sgt Bevins and to track down something to eat.

The second part of Max's life story was told the next day by Max himself. Flanked by Matron and the Headmaster's wife, he started with his memories from when he was about four, arriving on the Isle of Man with his parents to go to an amazing school. He'd lived on the school ground as his father was a teacher there. He'd never had any idea or inclination that there was anything wrong with his perfect life.

He loved his mum and dad, he had a great time at school, academically did very well and enjoyed the sports lessons.

It was only since enrolling in the cadets that he'd started to remember a different life and began having nightmares about it. He vaguely remembered a different father, and that there were uniforms and tanks and guns. He had night terrors when he would wake up screaming. Could the memories just be as a result of the dreams? He hadn't been sure. At the time it frightened him and his mother, but they hadn't known what to do about it. It was only now that someone had explained who he really could be, that the dreams began to make sense.

'What happens now?' Jeremy had asked, his eyes wide with terror. 'Are my mum and dad coming back? When can I see them?'

'Jeremy,' the Headmaster's wife spoke. 'Do you remember that yesterday the police sent someone to take a DNA sample from you by swabbing the inside of your mouth?'

Jeremy nodded. 'I didn't like it much.'

'No, I know, but that will help the police a lot. It will tell them who your real parents are.'

'I know, it's DNA isn't it? We did it in Mr Pope's class.'

'Yes, that's absolutely right. We should have the results as early as tomorrow.'

'What happens when we get them?'

Mrs Slater looked over at Crane.

'It means,' Crane explained. 'That you'll come back with me and Sgt Bevins here.'

Max frowned. 'With you two? Where to?'

'Back to Aldershot to see your mum.'

'You mean my mum's alive? My real mum?'

Crane nodded. 'The woman who could be your real mum, yes.' Crane knew this was all very confusing for the poor boy who was clearly still in shock, but he felt he had to get the distinction right. For who knew what the hell would happen if Jeremy Strickland wasn't Max Green and was someone else entirely.

Chapter 25

The following morning, Crane and Bevins were called to the police headquarters in Douglas.

'Ah, Crane, Bevins, thanks for coming. Please, sit. I'm DI Turner.'

In the corner stood their police liaison, who was clearly not to be part of the conversation, but just an observer.

'Right, well, we have the DNA results back,' Turner said.

'That must have cost, to get it back so quickly,' Bevins said.

'Quite. But the last thing any of us wanted was a protracted wait.'

'Indeed,' echoed Crane. 'So, what does it say? The DNA?'

'That Jeremy Strickland is one and the same Max Green.'

Crane realised he hadn't been breathing and sucked in a lung full of air. So, their suspicions had been correct. It was now time to talk about the boy's future.

'So, what happens now?' asked Bevins, before Crane could.

'There is obviously some paperwork to be taken care of. For the moment Mr and Mrs Strickland will continue to be held here at the local prison.'

'Ah, so that's where they are, I did wonder,' said Crane.

'Yes, they are. Both of them in the only prison on the island, but in different wings. There is one wing for men and another one for women. They will need to appear before the local Magistrate, who will decide what to do with them.'

'Send them to Aldershot?' asked Bevins.

'That's most likely,' agreed DI Turner.

'And Max?'

'Can go back with you. As the adoption was false, his birth mother is his legal guardian still. There's nothing to be gained by keeping him here.'

'Thank you, Sir,' said Bevins, standing. 'I'll go and make the arrangements.'

Crane stood as well and shook Turner's hand as they left.

'That went well,' he said to Bevins as they walked out into the Manx sunshine.

'Aye, as well as could be expected. Although God knows what it's done to that poor boy.'

'I think he'll need counselling,' said Crane.

'Absolutely. I can no doubt arrange it under victim support.'

'You're a good man, Bevins,' said Crane. 'You know you remind me of another officer from Aldershot Police.'

'Ah,' Bevins said as they strolled through the streets of Douglas. 'The redoubtable DI Anderson. Although I don't eat chocolate like he was reputed to have done.'

'No,' grinned Crane. 'I've never known anyone eat a bar of chocolate as quickly as he could. Let's grab a coffee, while we make the arrangements with Aldershot and with the Headmaster. I'm wondering if Matron could accompany Jeremy. Or Max as we ought to call him now.'

'Bloody good idea, Crane,' said Bevins.

'To which bit?'

'All of it. Let's start with the coffee.'

Chapter 26

Later that day, Crane was press ganged into talking to Jeremy Strickland, as he had a boy about the same age. Crane didn't think that helped any, but Bevins was determined not to be the one to break the news. So, once Crane had Matron onside, they went to talk to Jeremy together.

As gently as he could, Crane told Jeremy what had happened since he was about four years old. That he'd been taken from his mother, by his father, and supposedly sent to a posh boarding school. By a quirk of fate, that was exactly what had happened.

As Crane believed in telling the truth, he explained as clearly as he could, that his parents, George and Mavis Strickland had paid his abductors to get a child to adopt. However, that adoption wasn't legal and was infact illegal.

'Where are my parents?' Jeremy demanded.

'I'm sorry, lad, but they're in prison. They will appear before a local Magistrate who will decide if they stay here, or are taken to the UK.

'What about me?'

'You'll be coming with us back to the UK, to be reunited with your mother, Johanne Green.

'Will my father be there too?'

Crane shook his head. 'He's dead, we believe killed by the criminals who abducted you.'

Crane watched as emotions tracked themselves along Max's face. 'So what's my real name?' he whispered.

'Max. Max Green. You'll be coming back with me, Bevins and Matron here will come too.'

'When?'

'Tomorrow morning.'

'What if I don't want to go? Want to stay here?'

'That's not an option I'm afraid.'

Crane watched as Jeremy seemingly changed into Max Green. The boy fell silent. His face closed and became hardened. But it was his eyes that concerned Crane. They were staring at Crane with something akin to hatred.

All through the ferry and the journey back to Aldershot, Max said nothing. Not a thing. He accepted the food and drink given to him, but had little interest in it. He shrugged off Matron's gentle touches and even though he was in the midst of the group, somehow stood alone.

By the time they got to Aldershot, they were all exhausted. The journey had been a long one and Crane was so tired of trying to chivvy Max along. Max, of course, was having none of it. Crane began to dread the meeting with Johanne Green.

As Crane feared, when they got to Aldershot and Max met his real mother, he was equally silent.

'I'm sure he'll come round,' Matron said. 'It's all quite an upheaval for him. Just give him time.'

But the coldness Max displayed towards his mother was unnerving Crane.

Chapter 27

A few days later, Crane called in on Johanne Green and Max. He found the boy in his cramped bedroom in the flat that she rented. He was sat there, surrounded by his toys from when he was four. With an open suitcase abandoned on the floor. The image brought a lump to Crane's throat, to see a boy so very lost and upset.

'I'm sure the rest of your stuff from school will arrive soon,' Crane said.

Max said nothing.

'I'll be nice to have your own things and clothes back, I'm sure.'

'I'd like my parents back.'

'I'm sorry, Max.'

'Are you? Are you really? Why did you do it, Crane? I was happy on the Isle of Man. I've lost my mum and dad, my mates, my school, my future. For what? Aldershot? From what I can see it's the arse end of nowhere. I was loved and loved my life and you've taken it all away.'

Crane was taken aback by the intense feelings behind Max's words. 'For justice, son. That's why I did it. For justice. Isn't that important? To right the wrongs?'

'Well let me tell you, my life might have been wrong in your eyes, but it felt bloody right to me.'

Crane had no answer to that. He left the boy lying on his bed, facing the wall.

Seeing the boy's sadness and hatred of him, pierced Crane. All his life he'd worked so hard for justice. Had made it his life's mission.

But this time he had to wonder, had he got it wrong?

And if so, what did that do for the remainder of his career?

The End

A note from Wendy

Dear Reader

Welcome to the world of Sgt Major Crane and associated books!

At the time of writing, I've written quite a few series. There is the Sgt Major Crane crime thrillers, Crane and Anderson serial killer thrillers and now the Sgt Major Crane cold cases. There is also a supernatural police series featuring DI Jo Wolfe who can hear the dead speak, a cozy mystery series set in the fictional seaside town of Muddlebay and three Emma Harrison mysteries.

If you enjoyed this book, would you please consider leaving a rating and/or a review. This helps inform other readers when they are choosing what to read next and hopefully persuades them to try a new series.

Thank you for reading my books, it means more to me than you'll ever know.

Happy reading until next time.

Wendy

By Wendy Cartmell

Wendy Cartmell is a bestselling Amazon author, well known for her chilling crime thrillers. These include the Sgt Major Crane mysteries, Crane and Anderson police procedurals, the Emma Harrison mysteries and a cozy mystery series, set in Muddlebay. Further, a psychic detective series has been written, the first of which, Touching the Dead has been followed by six further books in the series. Finally, the haunted series is a collection of ghostly happenings in buildings or objects. Just click the covers to go to the book pages on Amazon.

Sgt Major Crane crime thrillers:

Crane and Anderson crime thrillers:

Emma Harrison mysteries

Supernatural suspense

Cozy mystery

Cold Cases

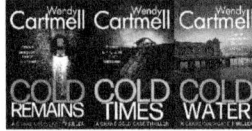

All my books are available to purchase or borrow from Amazon by clicking the covers.

Printed in Great Britain
by Amazon